ANDRES GALARRAGA

A Real-Life Reader Biography

Sue Boulais

Mitchell Lane Publishers, Inc.
P.O. Box 200 • Childs, Maryland 21916

First Printing

Real-Life Reader Biographies

Library of Congress Cataloging-in-Publication Data
Boulais, Sue
        Andres Galarraga / Sue Boulais.
                p. cm.—(A real-life reader biography)
        Includes index.
        Summary: A biography of the determined first baseman whose love of baseball brought him from the barrios of Venezuela to major league baseball first in Montreal, then with the Colorado Rockies, and now with the Atlanta Braves.
        ISBN 1-883845-61-0 (lib. bound)
        1. Galarraga, Andres, 1961– —Juvenile literature. 2. Baseball players—Venezuela—Biography—Juvenile literature. [1. Galarraga, Andres, 1961– . 2. Baseball players.] I. Title. II. Series.
GV865.G25B68 1998
796.357'092—dc21   97–43511
[B]   CIP
                                                                                                                                      AC

ABOUT THE AUTHOR: Sue Boulais is a freelance writer/editor based in Orlando, Florida. She has published numerous books, including **Famous Astronauts** (Media Materials) and **Hispanic American Achievers** (Frog Publications). Previously, she served as an editor for *Weekly Reader* and Harcourt Brace.

PHOTO CREDITS: cover: courtesy Andres Galarraga; p. 4 sketch by Barbara Tidman; p. 10 Otto Greule Jr., Allsport; p. 14 UPI/Corbis-Bettmann; p. 21 Stephen Dunn, Allsport; p. 24 courtesy Andres Galarraga; p. 27 Jed Jacobsohn, Allsport; p. 29 courtesy Andres Galarraga

ACKNOWLEDGMENTS: The following story is an authorized biography. It is based on contributing writer Tony Cantu's personal interviews with Andres Galarraga and has been approved by Andres Galarraga. It has been rewritten for a young audience by author Sue Boulais. It has been thoroughly researched and to the best of our knowledge represents a true story.

Table of Contents

Chapter 1
Dreams of Baseball

Andres José Galarraga was born in Caracas, the capital of Venezuela, on June 18, 1961. He is the youngest of five children. He has three brothers and a sister. His father, Francisco, was a house painter. His mother, Juana, is a housewife.

Andres can hardly remember a time when he did not dream of being a baseball player. He says, "I've loved baseball since I was very young. Ever since I was a

Andres always dreamed of being a baseball player.

child, I wanted to be a professional baseball player."

His family was not poor, but baseball equipment cost a lot of money. It was not always easy to give Andres the things he wanted. However, he was the baby of the family, and the older children often helped him get what he needed or wanted. "My brothers would help me out whenever I needed a glove, bat, ball, or uniform," Andres says.

When he was eight, Andres took the first step toward making his dream come true. He started playing as a first baseman for a team from his barrio, La Parroquia Chapellin, in Caracas. "We used to play barrio against barrio," he recalls.

When Andres wasn't playing baseball, he was watching baseball.

> **When he was eight, Andres played first baseman for a team from his barrio.**

Watching his heroes—baseball legends Reggie Jackson and Roberto Clemente—on television, he dreamed of being just like them someday. It didn't matter a bit to Andres that he was very far from the United States, where his heroes played. The major leagues of American baseball—that's where he wanted to be.

Andres kept playing baseball in his neighborhood in Venezuela, and he kept watching his heroes on TV. And, as he played and watched, he got better and better at baseball himself. He helped his team win several championships in Venezuela.

Although Andres played constantly, his family didn't know how serious he really was about the sport. After all, one of his brothers

His family did not know how serious Andres was about the sport.

When Andres was 18 years old, the Montreal Expos signed him.

had played for a while and loved it as much as Andres did, but he had quit. Andres, though, showed no signs of quitting. He kept loving it, day after day, game after game.

By the time he was 18 years old, Andres was so good that scouts from American ball teams were coming to Venezuela to watch him play. In January 1979, Andres took another big step toward his dream. The Montreal Expos signed him to play in their farm system.

Chapter 2
Making It Through the Minors

A baseball farm system trains young players who show skill and promise. If a player grows enough in skill and experience, the team manager may "harvest" him from the farm team and send him to play for the major-league team.

Just because a player is a member of a minor-league team does not mean that he will become a player in a major league. Some players spend their entire careers in

Playing in the minor leagues does not guarantee a major-league contract.

This photo was taken in 1990 when Andres played for the Montreal Expos.

the minor leagues. Andres knew he might never get to the major leagues. He also knew he had to follow his dream. "I didn't care about anything but playing," he recalls. "My family was in Venezuela, but I wanted to play baseball and this was my big chance."

The Montreal Expos first sent Andres to play on the minor-league team in West Palm Beach, Florida. He played just seven games there before he was transferred to the A-ball team in Calgary, Alberta, Canada.

Andres started off slowly with the A team, but he got better and better with each game. In his second year, his batting average was 49 points higher than that of his first year. By 1982, he had hit 14 home runs. That same year, he was moved back to West Palm Beach. Andres kept improving. By 1984, he earned the award for Most Valuable Player (MVP) in the Southern League.

But Andres was not satisfied with this honor—or with his progress. He wanted very badly to play in the major leagues. However, the Expos were hesitant to call him up. "They wouldn't sign me because they said I was fat," Andres says. "They had seen me bat, but they had their doubts. They thought that I would gain weight."

Andres wanted very badly to play in the major leagues.

At six feet three inches tall and weighing between 230 and 250 pounds, Andres is a large man. But he's not what you would call fat. In fact, he moves so quickly and easily that his nickname is the Big Cat, or *El Gato Grande* in Spanish.

Andres remained in the minor leagues for another year. Then, in 1985, he went to Indianapolis to play on the AAA team of the Cincinnati Reds. He played with enthusiasm and didn't let impatience hurt his game. His good behavior paid off.

Early in 1986, Andres got called up to the major leagues.

Chapter 3
At Last—
The Majors

Andres was just 23 years old when he went to the major leagues. During his years in the minors, he had married his high school sweetheart, a girl named Eneyda Rodriguez. The young couple had made a home in West Palm Beach, Florida. They were lonely—and they had trouble learning English. *"Dificilisimo* [very hard]," Andres recalls. "At first I felt different. I didn't speak any English. Everything was strange."

Andres had difficulty learning English.

_____
_____
_____

Andres tried to tag Tony Fernandez of the San Diego Padres when he attempted to steal a base on July 23, 1991.

But the move to the majors thrilled Andres. He was determined to make his dream of being a major-league ballplayer come true—and stay true. He slammed in 25 home runs and batted in 87 runs (RBIs). He played so well that year that the American Baseball Association

named him Rookie of the Year. (A rookie is a beginner.)

People in Venezuela watched Andres closely. They cheered each success in his career. Newspapers there often reported his achievements on the front page. In 1987, sportswriters in Venezuela voted Andres athlete of the year. When speaking with *El Mundo,* a Spanish-language newspaper in Florida, Andres said, "I always dreamed of getting this honor, and my dreams have been fulfilled. I'm a very happy man."

His successes continued. In 1989, Andres hit his first grand slam home run. (A grand slam is a home run hit when the bases are loaded.) Andres also earned his first Gold Glove award. The award was in recognition of his excellent

In 1987, sports-writers in Venezuela voted Andres athlete of the year.

performance at defense—catching balls and tagging batters out.

Andres performed just as well in 1990. He hit his second grand slam in August, the same month he had hit the one the year before. And he earned another Gold Glove Award.

El Diario of Caracas, Venezuela, often prints stories about Andres.

The move to the majors meant more attention and more success. It also meant more money. Andres and Eneyda were able to travel to Venezuela more often. On holidays and when the baseball season was over, the two would take off to visit relatives in Venezuela.

Those were good years for Andres. He enjoyed being honored in the United States, but he was even more proud of the recognition he received in Venezuela. When he was at home, he was mobbed by fans everywhere he went.

He was most proud of the recognition he received in Venezuela.

Chapter 4
Down and Out,
Then Back Again

In June 1991, Andres was hurt and could not play.

Too soon, though, it seemed to Andres that his happiness was over. In June of 1991, he hurt his left kneecap and couldn't play. For 36 games, Andres sat on the bench and watched his teammates. He hit only 9 homers in 107 games.

Thinking his best days were behind him, Montreal traded Andres to the St. Louis Cardinals for another player. After 13 years, Andres was no longer a member of the Montreal Expos.

Things got worse. His father died of cancer just a week after Andres joined St. Louis. A month later, his aunt, who lived next door to his parents in Caracas, died, too. Then, in the second game of the regular season, Andres was hit by a pitch that broke his right hand.

Andres felt very down. Between his sadness over the death of his father and the pain in his right hand, Andres played badly that season. For 44 games, he couldn't play at all. When he returned to play, he hit so poorly that the fans booed him. Joe Torre, the St. Louis manager, had to pinch hit for him. Andres was very embarrassed.

But there was no way that Andres would let the booing get to him. And there was no way that he was going to continue to let

Then his father died from cancer.

someone else bat for him. He says, "The negative things that happened to me were really a help. [The booing and embarrassment] made me work harder and try to improve."

The first thing Andres did to help himself was to ask for help from batting coach Don Baylor. The two men watched old films of Andres and decided that he should change the way he stood when he batted. Until that time, Andres had kept his legs fairly close together when he batted. He stood with his left foot much closer to home plate than his right.

After many sessions with Don, Andres started batting with his legs more spread out. In fact, the way he now stands at the plate is considered one of the most exaggerated open stances in baseball.

Andres also learned that his left eye was not as strong as his right. He and Don decided that he should turn his head slightly so that he directly faced the pitcher.

Andres stands at the plate with one of the most exaggerated open stances in baseball.

Both changes worked. In the second half of the 1992 baseball season, Andres had fully recovered from his hand injury. Up at the plate with his new stance, he became a powerful hitter again. In the final 45 games, he raised his batting average more than 115 points. He hit 8 home runs and 29 RBIs.

Still, because Andres had not performed well in the season's early games, St. Louis let him go. Now, Andres was out—out of job and, it seemed, out of luck. He no longer belonged to a baseball team, and it seemed no team wanted him.

Then Don Baylor, who had helped him so much during that tough year, got a job as the manager of the Colorado Rockies. The Rockies were an expansion team, a team that had begun because one of the major leagues decided it wanted to grow bigger. With Don as manager, Andres knew that he wanted to play for the Rockies. That wish came true on November 16, 1992, when Andres joined the team.

Even though Don believed in Andres, though, the Rockies were not sure how well Andres would do. They signed him for only one

Because he had not performed well early in the season, St. Louis let him go.

year at $600,000. Andres knew he had to prove that he could play well and be dependable in every game.

During the 1993 season, Andres played as he had never played before. He had to win back his reputation and win over his team. Not only did he raise his batting average another 69 points, he batted the best of all the league players that year.

What a comeback! Andres won the National League Batting Title, one of the highest honors in the major leagues. He became the first Venezuelan and the first player from an expansion team ever to win the title. His batting average was the highest by a right-handed batter in the majors since 1939—and the highest by any right-handed player at all since 1937!

Andres joined the Colorado Rockies and played as he had never played before.

His comeback included
another honor: Andres was chosen

to play in the All-Star game. He was the first representative from the Colorado Rockies to be picked for the game.

There was more yet to come. Since Andres had made such a spectacular return, his agent knew it was a good time to work out a new contract. Andres came out of the meeting with the team representatives with a four-year salary of $17.5 million.

The next four years were great ones for Andres. In 1996 and again in 1997, he led the Rockies with a batting average of .318, 41 homers, and 140 RBIs. In November 1997, the Atlanta Braves made Andres an offer he couldn't refuse. The Braves signed him to a $24.75 million, three-year contract. Andres had become one of the best players in all of baseball.

In 1997, Andres signed with the Atlanta Braves for an astounding $24.75 million, three-year contract.

Chapter 5
An Example for Young People

Andres has never forgotten his roots. He still prefers to speak in Spanish.

Andres celebrated his 36th birthday in 1997. Though many people think that he's too old to still be a professional athlete, Andres hopes to play until he is 40.

So, for the next several years, fans can find him where he has spent most of his career—at the plate hitting home runs or covering first base. That's right—Andres still plays first base, the position he has played since he was eight years old. He says, "I've also played third base and outfield. But I like first base the best."

Andres has never forgotten his roots. He still prefers to speak in Spanish. He remembers during his early years in the league that other

Andres and Dante Bichette trade congratulations.

Latino players helped him. When they spoke to him in Spanish, he says, it helped him get over his homesickness. He insists that his two daughters, who are bilingual, speak Spanish at home. *"Aqui se hable Espanol,"* he says. ("Here, Spanish is

spoken.") "In school, they can speak their language, but at home . . ."

Andres is also tremendously proud of his popularity in his home country. The most popular athlete from that country, his fans think of him as the Michael Jordan of Venezuela. They mob him whenever he returns there. The young people especially admire him. "I'm an example for them," Andres says proudly. "I'm the athlete [parents and teachers] name for children to watch."

Andres takes this role very seriously. With the endorsement of a beverage company, Andres visits schools and inspires young people all over Venezuela. He conducts baseball clinics, too, giving youngsters tips on their game. And, indeed, the young Venezuelans do

Andres is an example of what hard work and determination can do.

see in Andres an example of what they, too, can do with hard work and determination.

In fact, the admiration of his young fans was one of the reasons

In 1995, Andres launched his own line of sports apparel. He wants the children of Venezuela to be able to purchase merchandise with the name of their hero on it.

he launched his own line of sportswear in 1995. He wanted the children in Venezuela to be able to buy merchandise that had the name of their hero, *El Gato Grande,* printed on it.

Andres' love of baseball has never faltered.

From borrowing his brother's baseball uniform to launching his own line of clothing, the road from the barrios of Venezuela to the major leagues of the United States was not easy for Andres. Not all his years in baseball have been easy, either. However, his love for the sport has never faltered. He plays every game with the same eagerness and joy as he did when he was a child dreaming of being a professional ballplayer.

And that's the advice Andres gives to young people who want to succeed in life: "First, study and do what you love or what you're best at. Second, when you have the chance to do what you love, put your heart into it. Dedicate yourself to it. Do it with love and much enthusiasm so that your dreams are realized."

Chronology

- Born June, 18, 1961, in Caracas, Venezuela; mother: Juana Galarraga; father: Francisco Padovani Galarraga
- January 19, 1979, signed with Montreal Expos to play for their farm team
- 1984, married high school sweetheart, Eneyda Rodriguez
- 1985, called up to the major-league team of the Montreal Expos; named American Baseball Association's Rookie of the Year
- 1985, daughter Andria born in Caracas, Venezuela
- 1991, daughter Katherine born in Montreal, Quebec, Canada
- 1991, injured left kneecap; traded to the St. Louis Cardinals
- November 16, 1992, joined the Colorado Rockies
- 1993, won the National League Batting Title
- 1995, launched his own line of sports apparel and footwear
- 1997, hit 529-foot grand slam in game against Florida Marlins
- November 1997, signs with the Atlanta Braves for a $24.75 million, three-year contract

Index